Where Is My Mommy?

by Julie Downing

HarperCollinsPublishers

Where Is My Mommy?

Copyright © 2003 by Julie Downing

Manufactured in China. All rights reserved.

www.harperchildrens.com

Library of Congress Cataloging-in-Publication Data

Downing, Julie.

Where is my mommy? / by Julie Downing.

p.   cm.

Summary: Animal mothers, including a rabbit, cat, and human,
care for their young by waking them up,
washing their faces, and performing other activities.

ISBN 0-688-17824-3 — ISBN 0-688-17825-1 (lib. bdg.)

[1. Mother and child—Fiction.   2. Animals—Infancy—Fiction.]   I. Title.

PZ7.D75928 Wh   2003   [E]—dc21   2002068555

Typography by Stephanie Bart-Horvath

1 2 3 4 5 6 7 8 9 10

First Edition

To Anna and Will and my mommy

Where

is my

mommy?

She's waking me up.

Where

is my

mommy?

She's washing my face.

Where

is my

mommy?

She's bringing me food.

Where

is my

mommy?

She's playing with me.

Where

is my

mommy?

She's taking me home.

Where

is my

mommy?

She's waiting for me.

Where

is my

mommy?

Mommy is here!